Old Friends, New Friends

For my Dad—who treasures his friends,
old and new —P. H.

SIMON SPOTLIGHT
An imprint of Simon & Schuster Children's Publishing Division
1230 Avenue of the Americas
New York, New York 10020
This Simon Spotlight edition October 2015
Text and illustrations copyright © 2000 by Simon & Schuster, Inc.
The names and depictions of Raggedy Ann and Raggedy Andy are trademarks of Simon & Schuster, Inc.
SIMON SPOTLIGHT, READY-TO-READ, and colophon are registered trademarks of Simon & Schuster, Inc.
For information about special discounts for bulk purchases, please contact Simon & Schuster Special Sales at
1-866-506-1949 or business@simonandschuster.com
Manufactured in the United States of America 0915 LAK
2 4 6 8 10 9 7 5 3 1
Library of Congress Cataloging-in-Publication Data
Hall, Patricia, 1948-
Raggedy Ann & Andy : old friends, new friends / by Patricia Hall ;   illustrated by Alison Winfield.— 1st ed.
p. cm.—(Raggedy Ann & Andy) (Ready-to-read)
Summary: Marcella teaches Raggedy Ann and Raggedy Andy the fun of making new friends and the
importance of keeping old ones.
[1. Friendship—Fiction. 2. Dolls—Fiction.] I. Title: Raggedy Ann and Andy. II. Winfield, Alison, ill.
III. Title. IV. Series. V. Classic Raggedy Ann & Andy
PZ7.H147515 Raj 2002
[E]—dc21
2002000943
ISBN 978-1-4814-5086-7 (hc)
ISBN 978-1-4814-5085-0 (pbk)
ISBN 978-1-4814-5087-4 (eBook)
RaggedyAnnBooks.com

RAGGEDY ANN & ANDY
Old Friends, New Friends

Peachtree

by Patricia Hall
illustrated by Alison Winfield

Ready-to-Read

Simon Spotlight
New York   London   Toronto   Sydney   New Delhi

Marcella held Raggedy Ann
and Raggedy Andy
in her arms.

"I am meeting my friends
at the park!"
she said.

"Kate is my friend
from last year.
Lucy is a new girl in school,"

said Marcella
to her doll friends.
The dolls liked friends.

While Marcella waited
for her friends,
she sang a song.

"Make new friends,
but keep the old.
One is silver
and the other is gold."

Marcella ran to meet
Kate and Lucy.
"Can friends really
be silver?"
asked Raggedy Andy.

"Or gold?" asked the Camel
with the Wrinkled Knees.
"That must be people talk
for something very special,"
said Raggedy Ann.

Lucy and Kate
each held a doll.

"Oh, boy!"
whispered Raggedy Andy.
"We can make
new friends too!"

"Let's swing first,"
said Lucy.
"Then we can play catch,"
said Marcella.

"We can build
sand houses, too!"
laughed Kate.

The girls played together
all morning.

Then Mama called,
"Lunchtime!"

Raggedy Andy stood up.
"Hi, I am Raggedy Andy,"
he said.
He felt a little shy.

"My name is Bobby!"
said Kate's doll.
"And I am Alice!"
said Lucy's doll.

"I am Raggedy Ann.
I like your glasses."
"Thank you!"
said Alice.
"They are silver!"

"My name is Uncle Clem.
Your buttons are shiny."
"Do you like them?"
asked Bobby.
"They are gold!"

Soon nobody felt
shy anymore.
The dolls told stories
and they ran
and jumped around.

Alice picked some flowers
and gave them
to Uncle Clem.

Later the girls
played with their dolls.
Then it was time
to go home.
"Good-bye, Kate!
See you later, Lucy!"

That night
Marcella kissed her dolls.
"I had fun with
Kate and Lucy today,"
she said.

Marcella sang her song
again.

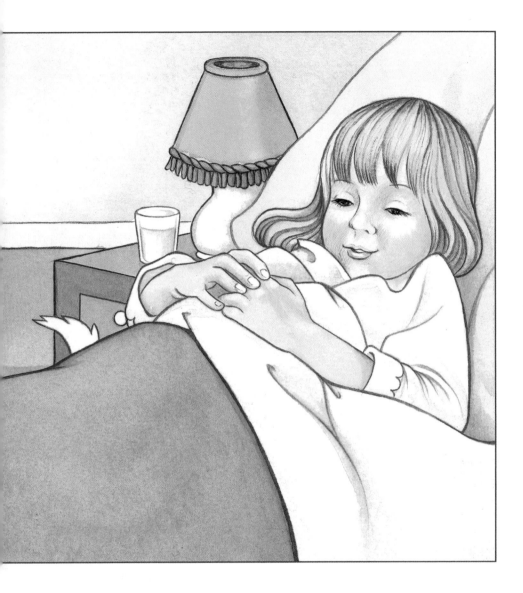

"Make new friends,
but keep the old.
One is silver
and the other is gold."

Later
Raggedy Ann
sat up in bed.
"I know what
Marcella's song means!"

she whispered.

"Silver and gold are different.
But they each are special."

"New friends and old friends
are different.
But they are each
special, too!

Just like all of us!"
Raggedy Andy giggled.

And with that,
all the dolls
fell fast asleep
to dream about
their old and new friends.